Aesop's Fables

Aesop's Fables rewritten and illustrated by Alice Shirley

First published in the United Kingdom in 2009 by

Pavilion Children's Books
10 Southcombe Street
London
W14 0RA

An imprint of Anova Books Company Ltd

Copyright © Pavilion Children's Books 2009
Illustrations © Alice Shirley 2009
Text © Alice Shirley 2009

The moral right of the author has been asserted.

ISBN: 9781843651185

A CIP catalogue record for this book is available from the British Library.

10 9 8 7 6 5 4 3 2 1

Reproduction by Dot Gradations Ltd, UK
Printed and bound by 1010 Printing International Ltd, China

This book can be ordered direct from the publisher at the website: www.anovabooks.com,
or try your local bookshop.

Aesop's Fables

RETOLD and ILLUSTRATED BY
ALICE SHIRLEY

PAVILION
CHILDREN'S

CONTENTS

THE GREAT RACE

Hare and Tortoise were arguing in the morning sunshine.

"I could beat you in a race with a broken leg!" Hare boasted.

"You may think that, but you're wrong!" retorted Tortoise. "I come from a family of great long distance runners. Think of how long we live for. I can easily outrun you."

"I'll race you then," challenged Hare.

"I'll race you across those four fields. We'll get spectators and judges to check for any cheating. And I'll win and show you how wrong you are!"

"Fine," replied Tortoise.

They had Goose give them the starting honk and the field mice to watch the checkpoints along the way. They had a flock of pigeons to hold up the finish line and wise old Owl to be judge. Many animals gathered at the finish line, all making bets as to who would win. Nobody doubted that speedy Hare was a sure thing.

As the sun climbed further into the sky, Hare and Tortoise lined up at the start. Goose honked as loudly as she could and they were off! Hare streaked ahead and quickly left slow plodding Tortoise behind.

Three fields ahead, Hare began to feel hot, running in the baking afternoon sun. Tortoise would not even get close for ages....Hare thought he would just take a rest under the hedge between the third and fourth fields where he was so close to the finishing line, he could get up and run as soon as he saw Tortoise coming. He lay down and waited...and waited. After a while he grew sleepy in the heat and fell asleep.

Meanwhile, at the finish line the pigeons cooed grumpily among themselves. They had been waiting for ages and thought Hare would have finished the race in minutes. They were sure they'd heard Goose honk the start...hadn't he?

Then they saw a shape coming very, very slowly towards them. As it came closer they saw it was Tortoise. They couldn't believe it! Hare was nowhere to be seen. Eventually Tortoise crossed the finish line and was declared the winner!

Hare woke, chilly as the evening drew in. He picked himself up and hurried off to the finish line...but everyone had long since gone to celebrate Tortoise's victory.

THE EAGLE
AND THE ARROW

Eagle flew high over the fields and forests, scanning the land for hares but he was spotted by a hunter. The hunter drew a feathered arrow in his bow, aimed and let the arrow fly. It pierced Eagle's breast and he let out a sharp cry:

"The feathers that steady the flight of this arrow to my heart have been plucked from the wings of an eagle! If only my feathers had made me safe in my flight!"

THE PEACOCK
AND THE JACKDAW

Peacock knew himself to be the most handsome and elegant of all of the birds. He spent many hours admiring his jewel-coloured iridescent feathers and crying out to anyone who would listen about his beauty. As much as he annoyed them, none of the birds could contradict him.

Peacock thought that he should be made King of the Birds and announced it at their next forest meeting. But Jackdaw let out a loud caw of disapproval: "Can all the finery Peacock has to offer protect us all from the talons of the eagle?"

THE HOUSE FULL OF MICE

The farm was overrun with mice, so the farmer bought a sleek black cat to catch them all. She twisted and pounced here and there, all teeth and claws. Most of the mice were killed, but some scurried back to hide in their holes.

Cat decided to hide from their sight to catch them by surprise when they came out to get food. She softly leapt up onto a dark shelf, hidden from sight. After a while a mouse crept to the mouth of his hole to see if the coast was clear. There was no sign of the cat on the floor, so he looked up – and out of the darkness of the top shelf gleamed the green eyes of Cat.

"Cat, I can see you waiting up there for me. I can tell you now that you will grow hungry waiting well before I come out of my hole to die at your vicious claws!"

THE GOAT WITH THE BROKEN HORN

The farmer asked his son to mind the goats and bring them in from the fields where they were grazing.

One of the goats was enjoying grazing on the juicy pasture and ignored the boy's calls to come into the pen. The boy got in a temper and threw a stone at the goat. The stone hit him so hard on the horn that it shattered and fell to the ground.

"Please don't tell my father," begged the boy. 'I'll be in such trouble!"

"I cannot hide your mistake," replied Goat. "It's obvious for all to see!"

THE FOOLISH DOG

A dog had found a huge chunk of meat decided to swim across the wide river, carrying it in his mouth to keep it away from the other greedy dogs.

At the banks of the river, he saw his reflection in the water and foolishly mistook it for another dog carrying an even bigger piece of meat. He leapt for it, but dropped his own piece of meat in the process. The meat was swept away in the river's current and the silly dog ended up with nothing.

THE PARROT AND THE CAT

A wealthy merchant bought himself a parrot from the bazaar and took it home, releasing it to fly freely about his home. He thought how wonderful and exotic it looked and loved the merry cackling noise it made. He fed it delicious nuts and berries. The merchant also had a cat that he kept in the house to keep the mice away.

Cat was very jealous of all the attention the newcomer got:

"Stop that ridiculous cackling! Why does the master let you chatter so freely, when he gives me a wallop if I utter a sound? It's so unfair!"

"Oh, don't be such a sourpuss," replied Parrot. "The master likes my chatter, but I don't think you could find a single creature that enjoys your yowling!"

THE ASS AND THE LAPDOG

A wealthy man who owned a large house and ran a successful business in town had a pet lapdog that he was very fond of. He would stroke it affectionately, throw balls for it to chase and feed it little treats. Its yapping and wagging tail made him happy when he returned to the house. The man also owned an ass that he used to carry his merchandise and shopping and for many other dull tasks.

Ass was envious of Lapdog's easy life and the affection that his master clearly had for it. He wondered if he behaved more as the little dog did, the master might treat him more kindly.

One evening, when his master returned Ass trotted up to greet him, braying and frolicking around him. Ass nearly trampled little Lapdog who had also come to greet the master and frightened the master as well, who was alarmed by the large creature kicking around all his precious goods in excitement.

The master ordered a servant to make sure the creature was tied up in the stable from then on and poor, jealous Ass was forced to live the rest of his days all by himself.

THE LION AND THE ELEPHANT

Lion was proud of being such a great and strong animal. As he walked among the other animals he knew that he was King of Beasts, no one could possibly rival him. However there was one thing that frightened him, that he never told any of the other animals about. He was too ashamed to admit it. He was utterly terrified of cockerels and shivered with fear just thinking about them. If he ever saw one, he pretended not to have seen it and walked rapidly in the opposite direction.

One day he was strolling through the grass when he came across Elephant, standing stock still, looking utterly terrified.

"What can possibly be bothering a great creature like you, Elephant?"

"There is a gnat buzzing near my ear!" whispered Elephant, trembling all over. "If it gets into my ear...I just couldn't stand it! The buzzing! And if I it died in there I could get an infection and then I would die!"

Lion smiled to himself, reached up and swatted the gnat away.

"Oh! Thank you! Thank you!" sighed Elephant in relief.

Lion walked away. 'A cockerel is far scarier than a gnat!', he thought to himself with satisfaction.

THE PEACOCK AND THE CRANE

Peacock was strutting across the lawn when he spotted Crane standing quietly at the edge of one of the garden fountains. The fountains were home to several plump koi carp and Peacock thought to himself that Crane was undoubtedly poaching.

He strutted to the fountain and flew up to the edge next to where Crane was standing.

"What are you doing here?" he demanded.

Crane was taken aback by Peacock's harsh tone. "I was merely lost in thought," he replied truthfully.

Peacock leant over and admired his reflection in the water.

"Such a pity you do not have such fine plumage, as I do," he sighed "It must be dull to be so drab all the time."

"Indeed", replied wily Crane. " Your feathers are most fine. However I can fly close to the Heavens and hear the songs of the angels. While I meditate on high thoughts you strut here on the ground, pecking and preening like a chicken!"

The Wolf and His Shadow

Wolf was walking in the evening sun to the river through a wide grassy meadow. Looking over one shoulder he noticed his shadow and thought about how enormous it appeared in the evening light.

"I am a great and fearsome beast. I have no fear of any animals – even lions and bears. I can fight them all off!" he boasted loudly to himself.

Little did he realise. Lion was lying in the grass not far off and had heard his foolish words. As he pounced on the unsuspecting Wolf, he growled into his ear:

"Luckily I am wrestling with your body and not your shadow!"

THE COCKS
AND THE PARTRIDGE

A man who kept some cocks on his land saw a partridge for sale at the market and put her among his cocks to feed her up. The cocks pecked and bullied her out of her grain, Partridge did not grow fat and the man never came for her.

Partridge assumed that they bullied her because her feathers, unlike theirs, were glossy, black and spotted.

As time went on, she saw that the cocks were as vicious with each other as they were with her. They pecked and scratched at each other in jealous fights – yet their petty bullying had saved her from the butcher's block.

THE CRAB AND THE FOX

Crab scuttled far onto the beach, scavenging for scraps. He decided that this was a much better place for looking for food than in the water because he didn't have to worry about all the other sea creatures snapping up the best morsels before he did. Fox came trotting along the beach and spotted a tasty morsel himself – the scuttling body of Crab. He pounced. Just before being snapped up by Fox's jaws, Crab cried out:

"Alas! Now instead of finding one, I am the dainty dish! I should never have left my home, the sea."

THE FLY

Fly was buzzing around the kitchen, being most annoying to the cook, who kept swatting at it. On the stove was a large vat of soup, simmering away for the afternoon meal. The cook made a swipe at the fly and sent it hurtling straight into the vat of soup. Fly swam in a few hapless circles before the warm broth began to drown him.

"Well at least I die happy," he buzzed to himself. "I have eaten and I have drunk. I have even bathed! Most of all, I die with the satisfaction that I have caused trouble for my enemy."

SOUR GRAPES

As usual, Fox was famished. As he trotted along the path keeping an eye out for any food, he spotted a vine that had climbed its way up into the branches of a tree.

Dangling tantalizingly just out of his reach hung a fat bunch of golden, juicy grapes. No matter how high he leaped for them, he could not reach the grapes. Turning sulkily back onto the path Fox muttered, "No matter...those grapes are probably sour anyway."

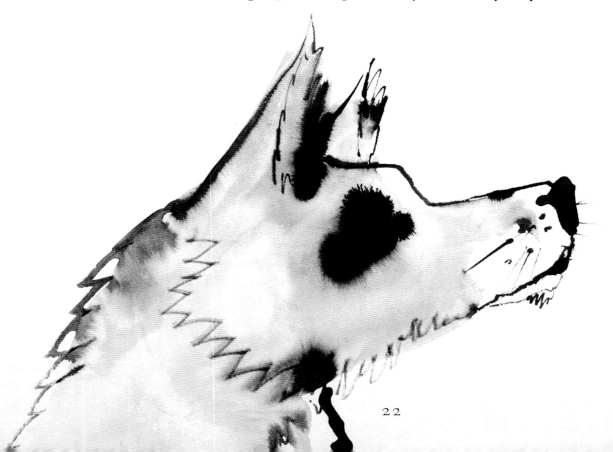

THE FERRET AND APHRODITE

A pet ferret was unfortunate enough to fall in love with a young handsome man who lived in the house next door. She longed to be transformed into a human so that he might be able to know her and perhaps love her too. She pleaded with the goddess of love, Aphrodite, to change her into a human. Aphrodite was so amused by this that she granted the little ferret's request and changed her into a beautiful young girl. The handsome man fell for her immediately and decided to make her his wife.

Aphrodite, however, was curious about whether the girl was still a little ferret in her heart. She sent a mouse scurrying into the young bride and groom's bedroom. The girl leapt and pounced on the mouse, catching it in her teeth without a moment's thought. The groom was horrified and left immediately, appalled by what had happened.

THE ASS AND THE HORSE

Ass looked gloomily over at Horse on the other side of the stable yard. It was just so unfair! Horse had the finest stable, delicious oats to eat, was groomed every day so that his glossy coat shone...he even had his own field to graze in. Horse never had to carry a load heavier than a man. Ass had to carry every heavy load around the farm, was given normal fodder to eat and beaten for any complaint or disobedience.

One day there was a great commotion. Bells were ringing in the nearby village, men were rushing to and fro along the roads and there were proclamations shouted. The country was at war and the farmer would have to fight. He saddled his horse and rode off to join in the battle.

Many months later the farmer returned thin and exhausted, leading along his lame horse back to the farm. The horse was thin and dusty, with many gashes and sores on his flanks.

Ass saw the sorry state the poor beast was in and his previous feelings of envy were replaced by pity. He knew now that Horse deserved his luxury.

THE EAGLE AND THE VIXEN

Eagle and Vixen became great friends and decided to live beside one another as neighbours. Eagle flew to the uppermost branches of a tall tree where she made a nest for her young, while Vixen burrowed a hole at the roots where she lived with her cubs.

One day when Fox was out scavenging for food, Eagle – who was also short of food for her chicks – stole one of Vixen's cubs to feed herself and her young.

Discovering the theft upon her return, Vixen was distraught, and driven mad by frustration. She wept bitterly: "My so-called friend has betrayed me! But how can I have vengeance on a creature of the air? I live on the ground!"

Yet Fate had listened Vixen's lament. Not two days later, Eagle was passing a village and saw that the men were burning the remains of a goat. She swooped down and carried it back to her hungry chicks. In her greed, she failed to notice that some of the skin was still alight. Her nest was made from twigs and straw and caught fire easily. The eaglets, still too young to fly away, were all burned to death.

Vixen, safe in her hole, smiled to herself with satisfaction.

THE WASP AND THE SNAKE

A snake was lying out in the sun basking, when a wasp came and landed on the top of his head.

The wasp stung the snake repeatedly, but no matter how hard the snake shook and twisted, he could not get it off. Snake was driven into a writhing fury, maddened by this torturous pain.

After a few minutes, Snake slithered over to a nearby pond and threw himself in the water.

Both Snake and his tormentor drowned in the stale water.

THE BEES AND ZEUS

The bees were furious! They toiled long and hard every day, but each time they made more honey, it was taken by the humans. They swarmed in anger, calling out for vengeance to Zeus on Mount Olympus.

Zeus listened with patience to the pleas of the bees swarming about his ear: "Oh Zeus, give us strength to avenge ourselves!"

Zeus did not like the thought of these creatures acting cruelly towards his beloved mankind. He knew how sweet the honey tasted, and understood why the humans kept coming back for more. He decided to grant the bees request, but at a price.

He gave every bee a sting, so they could protect themselves from human hands. Yet he made sure that when the bee used their sting, they would also lose their life.

THE INJURED WOLF AND THE EWE

Ewe was on her way to the stream when she spotted a wolf caught in a rabbit trap a little way along the hedgerow.

"My friend," he called out to her, "I have been caught in this trap all night and all morning. I am terribly thirsty. Hungry too. Would you be a dear, and go to the stream and bring me back some water. I am so terribly parched!"

"If I am to be the one who quenches your thirst, I will be the one to end your hunger also!" replied clever Ewe.

THE BAT AND THE FERRETS

A bat was flying about in the dim light of dusk. A small boy spotted it and threw a stone at the little creature. The poor thing dropped to the ground, stunned. A ferret came hurrying past on its way to the barn to hunt for mice and saw the bat sprawled upon the ground. Ferret pounced on what it thought was a very easy meal.

"Oh no!" cried Bat, "you don't want to eat me! I am a bird, not a mouse."

The ferret let the bat go, continuing on her way to the barn to catch mice. The bat managed to flutter back into the air and hurried home to recover from his ordeal.

A few nights later Bat was out flying at dusk. He was soaring around the treetops trying to catch moths for his supper. He misjudged a turn in the air and plummeted to the ground. A ferret, who was out hunting for little birds among the trees, couldn't believe her luck! She seized the bat in her jaws, but the bat flapped about in alarm.

"I am not a bird! I have no beak or feathers, look!" cried out Bat.

"Ah yes, you're right," said Ferret. "I will let you go – you are not the morsel for me."

THE FROGS WHO WANTED A KING

It is well known that frogs are simple creatures, with small needs. One day they decided that they could not continue without a King to rule over them so they went to Zeus – King of all the Gods – and demanded he provide them with a ruler.

Zeus was amused by the demands of these tiny creatures and threw a log into the pond, to watch their response. The frogs were startled by the mighty splash the log had made when it landed in the middle of their pond and sloped off to the murky corners of the pond to hide.

With time, the frogs became comfortable with the presence of their new King and, after approaching with some trepidation they soon realised they could leap all over him without so much as a grunt in response.

Gradually they realised that the log was not much of
a leader and grew discontented again. They went
back to Zeus, but he was no longer amused by
their requests.

He sent a huge serpent to the pond and not
one frog survived the new King's
tyrannical reign.

THE SATISFIED
WOLF AND THE EWE

Wolf had eaten his fill – three lambs, five chickens, two rabbits, three hares, and a duck. It was an astonishing amount and there was no way he could eat another thing...at least for a couple of days.

As he made his way back to his cave he came across a plump ewe, who had fallen over onto her back and could not get back up on her feet again. If he had not already eaten more than he needed, she would have been an easy meal. He couldn't decide whether to kill her anyway, just for the sport of it.

Wolf decided it was no sport without a chase. So he decided to let her choose her own fate:

"If you can tell me three truths, my dear, I shall leave you in peace. Fail to do so and I will kill you on the spot"

"That's easy for me," spat Ewe. "Unlike you, I am used to telling the truth! Firstly, I would never like to see you again. Secondly, if I did have to see you again, I wish that you were blind, so that you would not see me. Thirdly I would be overjoyed to learn that every wolf in the land met a violent death like the cruel fate they inflict upon their prey!"

Wolf, taken aback at such brutal truths, turned on his heel and left the ewe alone.

THE GOAT AND THE DONKEY

Goat envied all the delicious grain that Donkey was being fed as he worked on the farm.

"Poor creature!" she called out to him. "You work so hard all day long, carrying heavy burdens and toiling at the grindstone. You deserve a holiday. If you were to have a fall, you would get some proper rest."

Simple-minded Donkey thought what a fine plan this was, so he stumbled and fell, cutting and bruising himself on one side. The farmer saw Donkey's injury and asked the vet what he should do. The vet told him that drinking an infusion made from the lung of goat was the best cure for Donkey's bruising. The farmer reasoned that Donkey was far more useful to him on the farm and so slaughtered Goat in order to cure Donkey.

THE ANT AND
THE SCARAB BEETLE

Scarab was out sunning himself when he saw Ant hurrying past with a huge load of grains piled on his back. He was clearly on his way back to the nest.

"Why are you working so hard, Ant? It's the height of summer! You should be on holiday, relaxing! Look at me and follow my example."

Ant continued on his way, intent upon his work, not pausing even to look at Scarab.

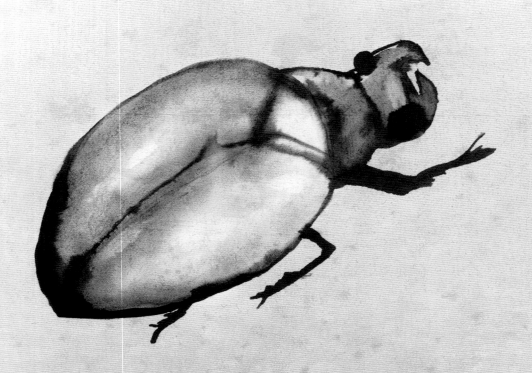

All too soon the seasons began to change. Heavy rains poured down, washing away all the dung that had been festering over the summer. The months got colder and colder and Scarab suffered and was hungry. He went to Ant to ask for some food.

"Sunning yourself all summer does not feed you all winter," said Ant to Scarab. "If you were wise, you would have followed my example."

THE ADDER AND THE FILE

Foolish Adder had a nest of little baby adders to feed. Needing someone to help with the feeding, she slithered into the nearest building – a blacksmiths – and went to each tool lined up on the workbench to ask if it could help her feed her babies. The hammer, the irons and the anvil all ignored her. Eventually she asked the file if it would give her anything.

"You ought to know," replied the file, "I am in the habit of taking away, not giving things. It is not in my nature."

The Fawn and the Stag

A fawn looked up at her father and asked him why he always ran away from the hounds.

"After all, you have a mighty set of antlers to defend yourself with! You have nothing to fear."

"It is true," replied the Stag, "but one set of antlers against a whole pack of dogs is not nearly as good as a swift set of legs to run away from them. I am lucky to have both!"

The Kite and the Snake

It had been a long afternoon and Kite was hungry. As she soared over the meadow, she spotted a snake moving among the grass. She dropped like a stone and snatched the snake in her talons. She realised too late that the snake was filled with venom and before she knew it, it had twisted around and bitten her!

"Serves you right," hissed the snake. "I have never done you any harm. You should have been more cautious before you attacked."

THE BEAR AND THE FOX

Bear was telling his friend Fox how he was a great friend of the humans who lived in the nearby village. "If I found a dead man in the forest, I would not think of eating him."

Fox was stunned: "If you would attack the dead rather than the living, then the humans might regard you as a friend to them too!"

THE MOUSE, THE FROG AND THE HAWK

Mouse and Frog decided that it was a good idea that they be the very best of friends. Little did they know what a terrible idea this was. To us it is really very obvious: frogs live in water, and mice live on land. They decided that the best way to be close friends was to tie a thread tightly to each others legs. This way they could never be separated.

They began their ill-fated friendship on the land, but soon Frog complained that his skin was getting dry and puckered from not being in the water. He leapt into his pond, dragging Mouse in after him. Croaking happily and swimming to soothe his skin, he did not notice that poor Mouse had drowned.

A hawk flying overhead saw the dead mouse in the water, dived and caught him in her talons. As she flew up, she hoisted Frog up and out of the water too.

"Two meals!" exclaimed Hawk, with delight. "When I was only hunting for one!"

THE CAT AND THE COCKEREL

Cat was prowling around the stable feeling famished, having not caught a single rat or mouse all day. She saw a flutter in one corner, pounced and surprised herself by catching Cockerel. Though she knew it was wrong, she decided to eat him, but thought she ought to have a reason to do so: "You crow most annoyingly in the morning, and wake all who hear your racket at dawn!" she hissed to Cockerel beneath her paws.

"I try to be a helpful alarm call for everyone. How else would you know to get up?"

"Well," Cat replied, searching for another excuse to devour him. "You spend far too much time with your hens!"

"If I did not there would be no eggs, nor chicks to grow into hens for the farmer to eat."

"Pah!" cried Cat. "You quibble beneath my paws, yet you are my meal already. I am a vicious creature and will eat you, no matter what you say!" So she made him her supper, feathers and all.

THE WILD ASS AND THE DOMESTIC ASS

A wild ass wandered onto a farmer's land and saw the farmer's ass grazing in a field of lush green grass. He noted how healthy and plump the domestic ass was compared to his own skinny frame. He had to forage on the scorched grass and tough heathers that grew on the hillside, while the domestic ass was fed every day by the farmer.

A few hours later the wild ass saw the farmer come striding up to the domestic ass and tie a bridle onto its head. He led the ass to edge of the field and began to load him with large heavy sacks of grain. While the ass was being loaded up it moved slightly away from the farmer, shifting from foot to foot. This made the farmer angry, so he took off his belt and used it to beat the ass until it cowered in pain.

"Ah," thought wild ass to himself. "I see that a life of luxury comes at a price."

THE FOX AND THE MASK

Fox was hungry and snuck into a nearby house to see what scraps he could find in the kitchen. He did not know that it was an actor's house and got a terrible fright from a hideous monster head sitting on the kitchen table. When its great eyes did not move, he took a step closer and realised that the head was, in fact, just a mask.

Fox smiled to himself:

"Such a scare would have got rid of a more timid thief, but I am clever enough to see this monster has no brain!"

THE WOLF AND THE HUNTING DOG

Wolf was trotting through the wood when he passed a large wooden hunting lodge. Chained outside the lodge was the largest dog he had ever seen. It had huge, whiskered jaws, large brown eyes and well muscled shoulders and was wearing a very heavy looking collar and harness.

"Who chained up such a magnificent beast?"

"My master. A hunter," replied the dog.

"Why did he chain you up? It must be very humiliating for you."

"Because," said the dog, "It prevents me from chasing after every beast that passes the cabin. Including you!" And he lunged at Wolf.

Wolf only just managed to leap out of the way in time and hurried off into the woods, amazed that another animal could be so vicious.

FOX'S CHOPPED TAIL

One night, when out hunting for rabbits in the forest, Fox caught his tail in a trap. Realising he would be left to die alone if he didn't free himself, he gnawed off the end of his tail in order to save himself.

However when he joined the other foxes back at home, he felt embarrassed about his injury. With an air of authority and confidence he called out to all the others:

"Really, it is so liberating to be without my tail! It was such a tiresome burden. I really look much better without it. I urge you all to do the same and get rid of your troublesome tails!"

"If you still had your own tail, I doubt your advice would be the same," his friends replied.

THE ASS AND THE MULE ON THE ROAD

Ass and Mule were trudging along the road from the port to the marketplace. Both were carrying the same heavy amount of salt and spices, but Ass complained that Mule was much stronger than him. He said that he should be carrying some of his load. Mule ignored him.

Further along the road the merchant driving them saw that Ass was struggling and transferred over some of his load to Mule. A few miles on it was clear to the merchant that Ass could not even cope with the smaller weight he now carried, so he moved all the salt and spices onto Mule's back.

"Well, in all fairness," said Mule to Ass, " I should now get fed twice as much."

He got what he wished for – the merchant sold the useless Ass at the market and he fed Mule all of the oats as a reward for his hard work.

THE JACKDAW AND THE BIRDS

One summer evening, Zeus announced that he was going to choose a King of the Birds the next morning: "Whoever looks the finest, with gleaming feathers and a sharpened beak will be chosen to rule the birds."

Upon hearing this, all the birds rushed to the riverbank to preen themselves for the competition. Jackdaw knew that he was dowdy and dull and could never hope to win. He went down to the riverbank anyway and saw all the multitude of coloured feathers scattered on the ground around the preening birds. Swiftly, he began collecting them up and sticking them in among his own feathers. Little by little, he acquired the most elaborate plumage ever seen. On the day of the competition, Zeus was filled with admiration for this exotic and unusual bird and named him King.

After the competition, one of the birds saw a patch of Jackdaw's colourful feathers were missing and saw through his disguise. Infuriated, the other bird began pecking out all of Jackdaw's fancy plumage. Seeing what was happening, all the others joined in. Soon Jackdaw was left alone, disgraced and plucked half-bald.

THE FOX
AND THE LEOPARD

Leopard was boasting to Fox what a beautiful coat she had, so sleek and with such wonderful spots in such dashing colours! Fox, who thought himself a most dashing creature, replied haughtily: "My beauty, unlike yours, is much more than skin deep! My beauty runs through to my very soul!"

THE FLEA
AND THE OX

Flea was resting on the head of the great Ox when he suddenly thought of a question.

"You are such a huge and powerful beast. Why do you work for the farmer? You plough his fields and pull his cart. What does he do for you?"

"He rubs my head," replied Ox "and he brushes my coat, which feels nice."

"How lucky you are that you are so big. Such caresses from your master would squash me in an instant!"

The Dolphins, the Whales and the Squid

Out in the great wide sea the waves were being frantically churned and splashed by the battle raging between the dolphins and the whales. Each side believed the sea belonged to them. In the midst of these angry waters, little Squid was tossed from side to side.

"Please stop!" he pleaded.

A dolphin turned to Squid and replied with anger, "We would rather fight to the death than have a little nobody like you tell us what to do! Don't interfere in things that do not concern you!"

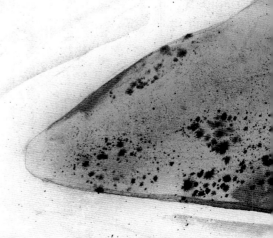

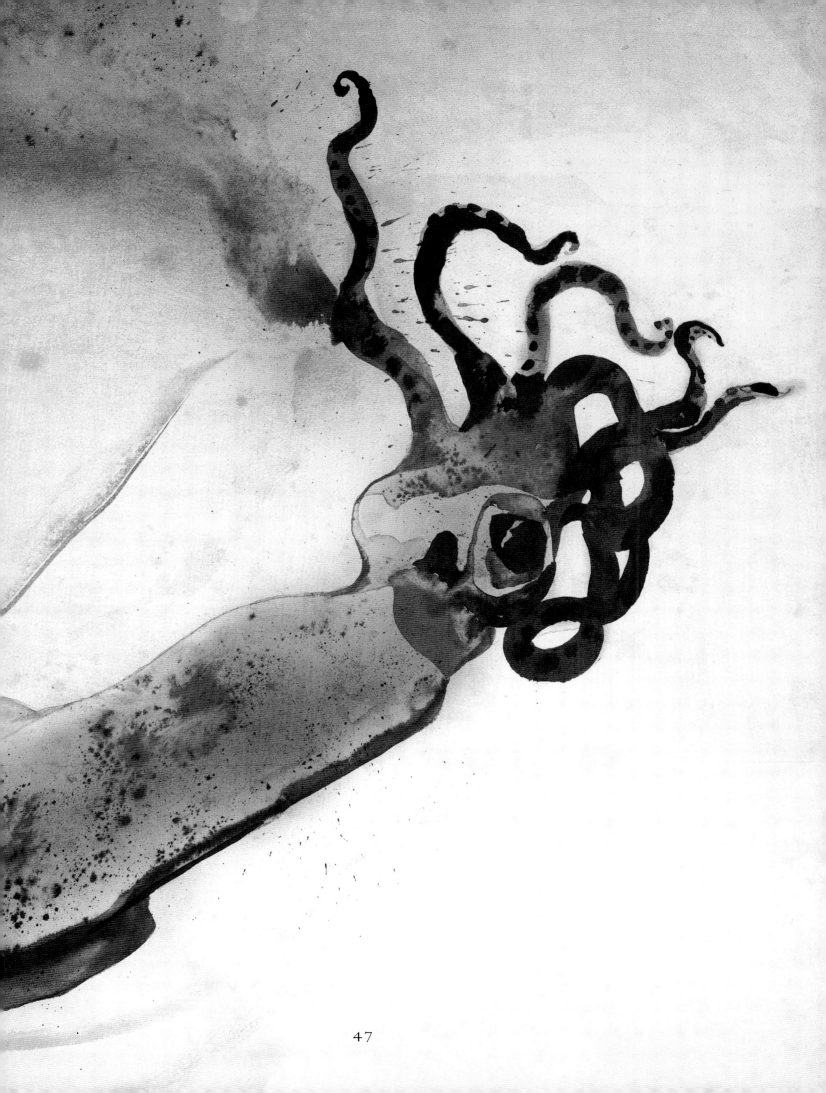

THE KID
ON THE ROOF

A kid managed to wander up onto the roof of a house, its little hooves trit-trotting on the tiles. He felt very pleased with himself. Down below he saw Wolf walking by and jeered at him: "Ha! you stupid old Wolf...can't get me up here!"

"Well," replied Wolf, "I do not think you would be nearly so cocky if you were within my reach."

THE PACT

The wolves were desperately trying to get into the sheep pen, but were prevented by the high fence and the dogs protecting the sheep. The wolves plotted among themselves and sent one forward to speak for them. The wolf cleared his throat and spoke to the dogs with confidence:

"Dearest dogs, we do not wish to be your enemies any longer. We are not so different, you know. We watch you and feel that you are not living your lives to the full. We are free animals that can do what we want and feast on nature's gifts, while you have collars and chains and are fed only scraps that your masters give you. You are slaves! Join us and we shall be a great pack together and roam wild and free. Let us in and we shall help you throw off your collars and chains!"

The dogs were convinced and let the wolf into the pen. All at once, all of the wolves flooded into the sheep pen. They fought the dogs off with their teeth before feasting on the sheep and lambs.

THE SCARAB BEETLES

On a little island lived a bull and with the bull lived two scarab beetles who ate his dung. As the cold of winter drew near and food had become scarce, one scarab said to the other:

"I will take a chance and hide myself onto the next boat to the mainland so that I can find some more food. You shall have plenty to eat if you are alone. I will bring back some food when I return."

The mainland had rich pickings and the scarab feasted all throughout the

winter. In the spring he returned to the island, with no intention of sharing with his friend.

"Why have you returned empty handed?" asked his friend, noting how fat and healthy he appeared.

"I'm glad to say that the mainland is indeed plentiful. But you cannot bring it back with you," replied the selfish scarab.

THE MULE

Mule was allowed to rest after many hard days work in the fields. He was given oats to get his strength back up, but these made him rather frisky.

"I bet that my father was a fine racehorse," he boasted to anyone who would listen. As a joke he was entered in a race with the farmer's horse. He lost by a long stretch and afterward looked very glum.

"I should have known that my father was really an ass."

THE NIGHTINGALE
AND THE HAWK

Nightingale was singing her usual beautiful song from a tall tree top. Hawk was hungry and tired and hearing her song, snatched her up in a sharp dive.

Nightingale let out the saddest song she could sing. "I am not enough of a meal for you, great Hawk. Let me go! I am sure that you will find a bird big enough for your appetite elsewhere."

To this Hawk replied: "A fluttering small meal you may be, but you are in my talons and the bigger bird of which you sing is not. I would be a fool to waste what I already have on the mere chance of more."

THE LION AND THE ASS OUT HUNTING TOGETHER

Ass thought himself a pretty tough creature – so tough in fact that he decided to ask Lion if he could join him when he next went out hunting. Lion was amused:

"Alright, but naturally I get all the spoils, agreed?"

"Agreed," replied Ass. "I just want to join you for the sport of it. Us tough beasts should work together."

They set off and followed a trail of hoof prints to a large cave. In it was a flock of wild goats. They put their heads together and Lion whispered a plan to his friend. Ass trotted into the cave and began to kick and buck and make a huge racket. The goats leapt aside and streamed out of the cave, straight into the waiting paws and jaws of ferocious Lion. After carefully picking off the choicest plump goat, he settled down to have his meal. Ass came trotting proudly out of the cave:

"Wasn't I brilliant? See how tough I am? They fled from me as they would from a tiger!"

"You fool," said Lion between mouthfuls. "They fled to avoid your mad behaviour. They know, as I know, that you are only an ass."

THE DANCING CAMEL

One day in the market place a merchant was trying to sell his camel. He commanded it to dance for a prospective buyer. Camel tried to dance, but naturally he was awkward and just stumbled about.

"This is a creature who cannot be graceful when he walks, let alone when he dances!" cried out the buyer.

THE TWO DOGS

A master bought two dogs from a farmer. He trained one to be a guard dog and the other as a hunting dog. Every time the master returned from hunting he gave a piece of meat to both the dogs as a treat. The hunting dog grew resentful about this. After all, he had done all the hard work to earn the meat. All the guard dog did was lie on his belly in the sun in front of the house all day and occasionally bark at people who passed by.

"Don't blame me for being the lazy creature that I am," said the guard dog. "Our master made it my job and it's your hard luck that you do not do the same."

THE NIGHTINGALE AND THE SWALLOW

"Why, dear Nightingale," asked Swallow "do you not live with me in the eaves and roofs of houses? It would be lovely to hear your song so close to my home!"

"Why would I want to live closer to those that wish to devour me?" replied Nightingale. "For there are many recipes for nightingale pie, but none for swallows!"

THE WILD GOATS

While out on the mountainside, a goatherd saw that some wild goats had mixed with his own flock. He herded them together into a cave to shelter for the night, where they stayed all together quite happily.

The next day, a terrible storm whistled and growled through the mountains. Unable to take the goats out to graze, the goatherd lifted a sack of grain and straw out of his bag. To his own goats he gave a handful each, but to the wild goats he gave a much bigger bundle, in the hope of persuading them to join the flock. They all passed another night in the cave, while the storm howled and raged and eventually blew itself out.

The next day was fine as the goatherd could have wished for. As soon as he let them all out, the wild goats ran and skipped off across the mountain. The goatherd shouted out how ungrateful they were.

"Wise, not ungrateful," replied the largest of the wild goats. "You only treat guests with hospitality and neglect those who loyally follow you every day."

THE LION, THE MOUSE AND THE FOX

Lion and Fox, who were good friends, fell asleep under a tree after their dinner together. Lion was purring a deep purring growl when he was suddenly awoken by something crawling across his full belly. He leapt up to see what it was and saw a mouse scuttling away through the grass. Fox had been woken by the commotion and began to laugh.

"You! King of Beasts, frightened of a tiny little mouse!"

"It wasn't that I was afraid! I was just surprised that any creature would dare to walk across the belly of a lion!"

THE FOX AND THE SHEEPDOG

A crafty Fox slipped in among a flock of grazing sheep without Sheepdog seeing him. In his rush to seize the fattest meal, he scared the lambs and their bleating alerted Sheepdog. Fox decided to pretend to cuddle the lamb.

"What are you doing with that lamb?" barked Sheepdog.

"I am just cuddling it!" said Fox, " lambs are so soft and sweet!"

"Well drop it," growled the dog, "unless you want me to cuddle you."

THE SONGBIRD
AND THE BAT

A caged songbird was hung out on the balcony of a house, so that her sweet voice could be heard in the courtyard and throughout the house. The bird refused to ever sing during the day, only at night.

Hearing Songbird's song one evening, Bat flew to her and asked her why she didn't sing during daylight hours.

"I was caught and put in a cage when I sang in the daylight" said Songbird, sadly. "I only sing now when I can be sure no one can see me"

"It is a bit late to be cautious," mused the bat. "I regret to tell you that the worst has already happened."

THE WEARY ASS

An ass was being driven to market by a merchant with several heavy sacks of salt upon his back.

After many miles of trudging slowly along the road to the town, they came to a river that had burst its banks. There had clearly been a heavy rain up in the mountains and now it was rushing down the rivers to the sea. The bridge to cross the river was still intact, but had a strong stream of water flowing over it. The merchant decided that they should cross it anyway and urged the ass forward. The water had made the bridge slippery and the ass stumbled half way across. As he fell, the sacks of salt slipped from his back and fell in the water. Naturally, the salt dissolved and the ass had nothing left to carry, so they turned and headed back the way they had come.

The next week the merchant was driving the ass on the road to town once again, only this time he had loaded him up with sponges. These were bulky, but much lighter than all that salt.

They arrived again at the river, which had gone down a bit during the night. The water was still flowing over the bridge, but not quite as fast. The ass and the merchant began to cross and the ass remembered the incident of his load disappearing.

He pretended to fall once again, but found that his load did not wash away this time. In fact the sponges soaked up a lot of water. The ass struggled to his feet again and found that his load was even heavier than all of the salt he had carried the previous day! He continued along the road to town with the merchant, burdened by the weight of his foolishness.

THE CICADA AND THE FOX

Cicada was singing her joyful summer song in the top of a tall poplar tree when she was interrupted by a voice from down below.

"My dear sweet singer!" said the voice, "I cannot see you, but I would dearly love to meet the possessor of such great musical talent."

Peering from behind a leaf, Cicada saw Fox below. He was always up to crafty tricks and she did not trust him one bit!

Cicada called out: "Here I come!" and threw down a leaf which fell near Fox's feet. He immediately pounced on it. He had intended to eat her all along.

"Why, is that how you treat all musicians that you love, or just me?" Cicada called out to him, safely up in the treetop.

THE EAGLE, THE JACKDAW AND THE SHEPHERD

Sitting on his fence post one fine spring morning, Jackdaw saw eagle carry off a young lamb for his meal. Jackdaw thought how grand it would be to have fresh meat himself, instead of scavenging for leftovers. He flew in circles over the flock, searching for a meal to satisfy his hunger. There were plenty of fat lambs, but he fancied a bigger meal for himself. He spotted a curly-horned ram among the ewes, which he decided would be just the feast for him. The closer he got, the bigger the ram appeared to be. It was enormous! He stretched out his claws which sank deep into the ram's thick wooly coat but he got stuck!

"You have certainly plucked more than you can peck!" said Shepherd as he wandered over. "You will make a fine foolish pet for my children." With that he clipped the bird's wings, tied a string to its leg and carried it home.

THE THREE BULLS AND THE LION

Lion was hungry and by some luck, he came across three bulls grazing in a field, one grey, one brown and one black. As he carefully approached them to attack, the grey bull saw him and encouraged the others to all stand close together. No matter which way he approached, Lion was confronted with hooves or horns and could not catch even one bull for his supper. So he went home hungry.

The next day he came back to the field and called out to the black bull:

"Your friends think you are weak and only stick with them because you are not brave enough to face your fears alone."

Then the lion went away again. The black bull was tormented by Lion's jibes. Determined to prove his former friends wrong, he stalked off to another field to graze alone.

Lion had been hiding to see his words take effect and followed the black bull. When they were out of sight of the other two, he pounced and feasted on the black bull.

The next day Lion went to the field and called out to the brown bull:

"I heard that your friend, the grey bull has been boasting to the other animals that he is of far superior breeding than you and only stays with you out of pity!"

The brown bull was hurt at these words and moved away from his companion to another part of the field. The grey bull's back was turned and he did not see the sorry fate of his friend, who was quickly devoured by Lion.

The next day Lion knew there was no need for taunts as the grey bull was left alone. He had no friends left to protect him. He would be an easy meal.

THE LION AND THE CHEETAH

Lion and Cheetah started chatting one fine morning and decided that together they would make a great hunting team. Lion was powerful and strong and could bring down even vary large creatures. Cheetah was faster than any other creature and could catch even the swiftest deer. They set out together, stalking and catching many unfortunate beasts. Truly they were a formidable team.

After only a few hours, they decided they had caught more than enough to satisfy them. Lion said he would divide the spoils. He gave himself a lion's share and flung a rabbit for Cheetah to have. Before Cheetah could argue, Lion growled low and dangerously:

"You are lucky that you too are not on top of my share. Take what you are lucky enough to get and get lost!"

Skinny Cheetah decided not to argue. He was no match for Lion's powerful muscles and jaws.

THE ANT AND THE PIGEON

Ant was busy gathering grain and juicy leaf buds in the warm spring sunshine. Suddenly the sky darkened and the Heavens opened. Rain fell from the skies as Zeus poured sheet upon sheet of rain upon the ground.

Poor little Ant was washed away and would surely have drowned, had a plump wood pigeon not seen her from the shelter of a tree. She swooped out into the rain to throw Ant a twig, which she could float on until the rains ended.

A few days later Ant spotted a hunter poised by the same tree, waiting for Wood Pigeon to fly away. Ant scuttled over to the poacher and bit his foot as hard as he could. The poacher jumped up and yelped in pain, thus alerting Wood Pigeon to his presence.

Wood Pigeon escaped, happy that his good favour had been returned.

THE MONKEY
AND THE CAMEL

Monkey loved to show off to all the other animals – telling jokes, playing the fool and dancing about, much to their endless amusement. One day as Monkey cavorted about, Camel, envious of all the laughter and attention that monkey received, got up and began to dance. He was so graceless and clumsy that he barged into Bull, trod on Tiger's tail and walloped Wolf in the face. The other animals were so angry that each of them shouted angrily at Camel.

Feeling foolish and miserable, Camel ran away into the desert, never to return.

THE JACKDAW AND THE FOX

Jackdaw was hungry and noticed some figs growing on a tree. As he flapped down to eat them, he noticed that they were not yet ripe. He settled on the branch sat there waiting for them to ripen.

Many hours later, Fox came trotting by and noticed Jackdaw perched wearily on the branch. He asked him what he was doing and when he was told, called out:

"You cannot fill your stomach with hope! Better that you know this, than die of hunger because of it."

THE SHEARED SHEEP

It was late in spring and the days were getting longer and warmer. The farmer decided it was time to shear the sheep of their old winter wool. He asked the stable boy to give him a hand with the shearing. The lad took hold of one of the sheep and set to work, but he was clumsy and kept nicking the poor creature's flesh with the shears. Soon Sheep had cuts all over his body.

"I wish you'd decide whether you want my flesh or my wool," he winced. "Your indecision is complete torture."

THE ASS AND THE FROGS

Ass was making her way to market across the vast wetlands, with several heavy loads of grain upon her back. She was negotiating her way around a bog when she slipped and fell into the mud. Struggle as she might, she could not get up – the mud was far too thick. She began to bray mournfully and loudly, thinking that she would be stuck there forever. A group of frogs in the bog heard her.

"Peace!" they croaked, "you've only been here a few minutes, yet you complain as though you have lived here as long as us!"

THE CRACKED CROCODILE

Fox and Crocodile were having a debate as to which of them came from a nobler heritage.

Crocodile boasted, "I come from a rich line of skilled athletes." He stretched out to his full length and said: "See my abilities? My ancestors were the greatest athletes in all the land."

"I can see that you have been overdoing it for quite some time," replied Fox. "Looking at the state of your skin, it is clear you have cracked yourself!"

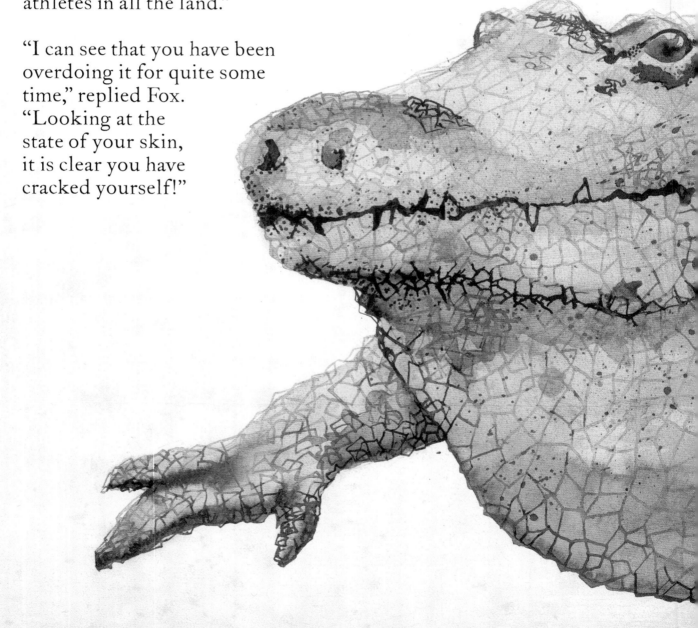

The Camel, the Elephant and the Ape

The animals were discussing who should be the next King. Both Camel and Elephant thought themselves very worthy candidates, due to their size and strength. But Ape pointed out that both had faults that made them unsuitable to be King:

"Camel," said Ape to the gathered crowd, "is unworthy because of his foul temper. He is unjust and cannot be trusted to rule with an even hoof. Elephant, on the other hand, is terrified of mice. If he flees from such a defenceless animal, how could we expect him to defend us against more ferocious beasts?"

The Frog Doctor

Frog had been reading a book on medicine and decided that he was now an expert on healing. He stood up on a soapbox and declared his great healing abilities to all the other animals.

"I can cure any illness, I have every lotion, potion, pill and tonic for you!"

Upon hearing this, Fox called out to Frog: "If you can cure any illness, why does your voice still croak?"

75

THE MOLE
AND HIS MOTHER

It is a well-known fact that moles are blind due to their years spent underground.

Two moles, a mother and her son, were burrowing through the ground underneath a storehouse. As they surfaced, the young mole exclaimed excitedly that, for the first time in his life, he was able to see!

"Oh Mother!" he exclaimed, "it is so bright and I can see so clearly!"

The mother mole bumbled over to a small sack and lifted out a grain and handed it over to her son.

"If you can see, then tell me what this is," she said.

"It is small, round and hard. It's a pebble," he said with certainty.

"Foolish boy!" Mother Mole retorted. "It is wheat. It seems that you are not only blind, but have lost your sense of smell too!

The Eagle and the Scarab Beetle

Hare was exhausted! He had been running from Eagle for many miles across the fields. He fell down in the shade of a rock and found himself face to face with the shiny Scarab beetle.

"Oh, Scarab! Help me! I'm sure I shall die! Eagle wants to eat me."

"Have no fear, Hare," she said soothingly. "Eagle is my friend and will listen to me."

She clicked her shining beetle wings when Eagle flew down to the rock, so as to draw her attention. "Dear Friend, please spare Hare! I beg you! You shall be rewarded for your mercy."

Eagle was full of disdain for such a small and insignificant creature. She just screeched, picked up Hare and ate him for dinner.

Scarab was furious and swore to have her revenge on the great bird and her family. She travelled to Eagle's nest high in the mountains and scuttled into it. She then rolled and pushed each and every egg out of the nest, which smashed onto the rocks below.

Seeing the smashed eggs on her return, Eagle was heartbroken. She learnt that she should listen to all of the other creatures, no matter how insignificant they seemed to be.

THE LION, THE FOX AND THE STAG

Lion was a mighty ruler over all the animals, but his power had made him rather lazy and he liked to get Fox to carry out tasks for him. One day he said to Fox: "I fancy eating Stag for my supper tonight. Will you bring him to me?" It was not a request. It was an order. Fox trotted off to the woodland where Stag lived, desperately thinking of how he could get Stag to come of his own accord. Fox knew he was not nearly strong enough to force him there. After some searching, he found Stag eating acorns under an ancient oak tree.

"My dear Sire," bowed Fox. "Let me please salute my future King."

"What on earth are you talking about?" asked Stag.

"Lion is dying. He has dismissed all other candidates for his crown, but you. He says that Wolf is too ruthless, that Bear is too irritable, that Boar is too stupid and that Tiger is too boastful. He says only you are suitable and he wishes to counsel you before he dies. He told me to bring you to him immediately."

Stag straightened up with pride, his great antlers catching the sunlight. He followed Fox back to the cave where Lion lived. As he entered the cave Lion leapt at him, but Stag was too quick and managed to leap aside. He bounded away, blood pouring from a gash that Lion had made with one of his claws. Lion was furious that he had missed his mark and turned on Fox:

"Go and get him back! If you can't then don't bother returning! And consider yourself my supper if I ever see you again!"

Fox knew his life depended on him thinking of a plan. He ran for miles, following the spots of blood on the grass, all the while trying to hatch a plan. Eventually he reached a very dark part of the woods where he found Stag resting, his great chest heaving. When he saw Fox he lunged at him with his antlers, but missed.

"Really, my dear Stag!" cried out Fox. "Do not kill the messenger! Lion was merely trying to whisper his instructions to you in your ear. His voice is weak because he is dying. You are frightened away by one little scratch from an ill and aged lion! He is furious and is now seriously talking about making Tiger King after all. If you come back right now and apologise to him, he might forgive you."

"Oh no!" cried Stag, horror struck, "I've ruined my chances!"

They hurried back to Lion's cave and entered. This time Lion did not miss his mark and killed Stag. As he devoured every last bit of him, Fox leapt out and snatched the heart and wolfed it down. He was determined to get some reward for all his efforts, even if it was not given freely. Lion looked around for his favourite morsel; he was very fond of heart. When he asked Fox where it had gone, Fox replied:

"I doubt such a foolish creature had one. If he had, it might have warned him not to walk straight into the paws of a lion, not once, but twice!"

THE FLIES AND THE HONEY

Out in the farmyard one sunny day, a farmer was loading several jars of honey onto a cart to take to market.

One of the jars of honey slipped from his grasp and smashed on the floor. Instantly, a swarm of flies gathered, attracted to the sweet smell of the honey oozing on the ground. They began to feast, but when they tried to move, they found that their feet were stuck in the oozing mixture.

The flies realised their greed had brought them to a sticky end.

THE CICADA WHO SANG ALL SUMMER

It was deep in the middle of winter and a hungry cicada came across an ants nest. He knew that ants were clever creatures. They worked busily all through the summer storing up food to eat in the colder months when food was scarce. He went up to a group of ants and asked if he might have some of their food. The ants asked him why he had none of his own food for the winter.

"Because I was singing all through the summer months," replied Cicada.

"If you were so stupid to spend your summer singing," jeered the ants, "then you can spend your winter dancing! You need to learn that neither of these frivolous pursuits will fill your belly."

THE SNAKE AND ZEUS

Snake was fed up. He lived by the side of a goat-track and was always being trodden on and kicked by their clunky hooves. He went to Zeus to seek his advice.

"If you had bitten the very first creature that had stepped on you," said Zeus, "then you would never have been trodden on a second time."

FOX AND THE BRAMBLE

Fox was an agile creature most of the time, but one wet day he slipped as he jumped from a stone wall. As he fell he reached out and grabbed what was nearest to him. Alas! This was a bramble and its thorns and spikes dug into his soft paws and made them bleed.

"Curse you!" he shouted at the bramble, "I reached for you to help me as I fell and instead you have injured me!"

"Well" bristled the bramble, "you reached out to me! You should know it is my instinct to climb all over others to support me and never offer support myself, nor encourage it, as you have discovered."

THE STARVING DOGS

A ragged pack of stray, hungry dogs saw some pieces of meat being dried out in the sun on the other side of a wide river.

One of the dogs had the idea that if they worked together they could drink up all the water that separated them from the meat.

They drank and drank, a row of pink tongues lapping at the water, but the river did not shrink even slightly.

The dogs, however, grew larger and larger. They drank and drank until their bellies were so full they could hardly move.

THE MONKEY
AND THE FISHING NET

Monkey was perched up in a fig tree, plucking the fruit from the branches and popping them whole into his mouth. They were deliciously ripe and juicy.

Below him was a rocky beach on which some fishermen were wading out in the water fishing with a net spread between them. After some time they decided to stop for lunch, before going back to work. They brought the net out with them, spread it on the rocks and walked away.

Monkey decided that he would most definitely be a much better fisherman than those fools! He scampered down his fig tree, across the rocks to the net. He held it up and began to drag it to the sea. Just then one of his feet got tangled in the net. As he tried to free himself, his tail got tangled too. Soon he was so tangled up in the fishing net he could barely move. After a while the fishermen returned to find a very strange fish in their net!

"What a fool I am!" cried Monkey. "I like to eat figs, not fish. I should not have strayed out of my tree, where I belong!"

THE TORTOISE
AND THE EAGLE

Tortoise had some very ambitious ideas. He wanted to fly like a bird so he could see high above the land and sea.

One day Eagle was resting on a rock near Tortoise, cleaning her talons.

Oh, Eagle!" exclaimed Tortoise, "How I would love to fly like you! How wonderful to be able to soar through the air! Instead of plodding along on the ground as I do."

Tortoise, you are not a flying creature," said Eagle. "You will never fly. For one thing, you don't even have wings!"

"Oh, but if you took me in you talons you could carry me" he pleaded, "I could swoop high above the mountains and deserts!"

After much persuading and bribery, Eagle agreed to fly with Tortoise up into the sky.

Up they soared and Tortoise let out many cries of delight! It was amazing to be up so high with the sound of the wind whistling through Eagle's feathers. Down below Eagle spotted a rabbit hopping across a field. She turned sharply and let go of Tortoise, diving down after the rabbit. She realised her mistake too late and Tortoise fell to the ground below.

THE JACKDAW
AND THE RAVENS

Greedy Jackdaw always took more than his fair share of the food. He grew much bigger than all of the other jackdaws.

Deciding that he was a cut above the company, Jackdaw flapped off to join the ravens.

The ravens did not want the foolish bird around and mobbed him when he came near them, so he was frightened away.

Defeated, he returned to the other jackdaws but they were offended by his desertion and refused to allow him to join them again.

Silly Jackdaw was condemned to a life of loneliness, unable to find even one friend.

THE NEIGHBOURING FROGS

One frog lived safe and sound in the bottom of a large pond, while her neighbour lived on the very edge of the path nearby.

"Why don't you come and live in my lovely big pond, there is plenty of room for both of us."

"Oh no, my dear!" replied her anxious neighbour. "I could not possibly leave my home. I am comfortable where I am."

The very next day a chariot came charging up the path towards the nearby town and before the neighbour could leap out of the way, she was squashed flat.

THE OXEN AND THE AXLE

Two oxen were ploughing in a field and every time they strained to pull the plough, the axle of their yoke would screech in protest.

"Axle," they chimed, "why do you complain so loudly when we are the ones doing all the hard work?"

THE LION AND THE WILD BOAR

The hottest, longest days of summer had begun. The river bed was cracked and dusty and the great lakes dried up to muddy puddles.

Lion and Wild Boar had been walking together for miles, trying to find water and they were both driven half mad with thirst. After many hours trudging, Boar sniffed at the air with his bristly snout and caught a whiff of sweet water. Eventually they found its source – a tiny spring bubbling up through the rocks.

There was only enough room for one of them to drink at a time and immediately a quarrel broke out as to who would be first to drink. Both Lion and Wild Boar were so desperate that they exchanged blows. Soon the fight escalated and it became clear they were going to kill each other.

Lion happened to look up and saw a crowd of ravens and vultures gathering on the branches of a nearby tree. They were waiting to devour whoever was killed first.

"Friend, we will both be a meal for that flock if we continue to fight! Let us be friends and both drink our fill."

THE WILD BOAR
AND THE FOX

Fox was trotting through the woods, searching for tender young hares when he heard a curious rasping noise.

It was certainly not the sound of trees being chopped down or cut up. It was not the sound of Lion crunching up bones. Fox followed the sound through the undergrowth until he came to an outcrop of rocks. On the other side was a great bristly wild boar, sharpening his tusks on the rock. So that was what the sound had been!

"Why are you sharpening your tusks, dear friend?" asked Fox.

"To protect me from huntsmen, dogs and other hungry beasts after my flesh," grunted Boar.

"But none of them are around today," said Fox. "The woods are quiet and peaceful today."

"Today is not tomorrow and who knows what that shall bring? I'd rather be prepared in the present, than be full of regrets in the future."

The Deer and the Vine

Deer was fleeing from some huntsmen who were pursuing her. She leapt into a vineyard and hid behind some overgrown vines. As she knew she could not be seen, she relaxed and waited, nibbling at the lush leaves around her. They were so delicious, she found she could not stop and before long, gaps began to appear in the thick vines that had covered her.

One of the huntsmen spotted the deer hidden in the vines and shot an arrow, striking her. As she fell she cried out:

"It is my own fault for destroying that which would have protected me!"

THE WOLF AND THE NANNY GOAT

Wolf was on his way back to his cave when he spied Nanny Goat grazing on the sparse tufts of grass growing on top of some rocks. She looked plump and delicious to Wolf and he thought she would make an excellent snack. But Wolf knew that while he was clumsy on the rocks, goats were renowned for their rock-climbing skills and would there was no chance he could sneak up her without her noticing. He would have to find a way to get her to come down.

"My dear friend," he called out to her, "you really must try the grass down here. This meadow has the sweetest grass, nourished by the freshest spring water. That scratchy tough stubble you are eating cannot be good for your stomach!"

"Ha!," replied Nanny Goat, looking shrewdly down at Wolf, "I shall be the judge of what is good for me to eat. Up here I am well nourished. You are only able to see what would be good for you to eat. I think I am quite happy where I am."

THE BOASTFUL
MONKEY AND THE FOX

Fox and Monkey were walking along together, engaged in a heated debate over who had the richer history in their family. Fox had just said that he was certain that his grandfather had been a Duke who had fought numerous brave battles for his King.

"My forefathers were great leaders and freedom fighters who died fighting for their beliefs. That is where they now rest!" Monkey blurted out, pointing as he did to some very impressive tombs that lay some distance off.

"How convenient that they are not able to arise and contradict your boasts," replied Fox with a wry smile.

THE RAGING LION
AND THE STAG

Lion was out hunting across the hills when he cut his paw on a sharp piece of flint hidden in the grass. He was enraged and snarled with fury that he, the King of Beasts, could suffer such a silly injury. All the hills and valleys echoed with his roars.

Stag heard his fury and warned the other animals:

"Lion is dangerous enough when he is calm! Pity us poor creatures who will suffer him in his wrath!"

ZEUS AND THE TORTOISE

Zeus, King of the Gods, had invited all the animals of the kingdom to his wedding feast. There was much merriment and joy among all the creatures and Zeus swelled with pride. Yet the following day, Zeus realised that Tortoise had not been there. He was outraged and stormed up to Tortoise, demanding an explanation.

"There's no place like home," replied Tortoise, nonplussed.

Zeus was infuriated with this remark and as a punishment, gave Tortoise a shell that he would have to carry on his back for the rest of time.

The Tuna Fish
and the Dolphin

Tuna was swimming as fast as he possibly could, to avoid becoming a meal for the hungry dolphin pursuing him. In one last effort not to be eaten, the tuna threw himself high up onto the beach. Without thinking the dolphin leapt too – high onto the beach and fell next to the tuna, who was gasping in the open air.

"At least I die with some satisfaction," gasped the tuna. "That my enemy should die as I do."

The Hen, the Swallow and the Eggs

Hen saw a nest of eggs lying abandoned near a hedge. The farmer always took her eggs away before she had a chance to hatch them and she desperately wanted to be a mother.

She decided she would hatch the abandoned eggs herself and settled down to keep them warm. Swallow was soaring over the grass catching flies to snack upon. He saw Hen settling on the eggs and called out to her in alarm:

"What are you doing!? Can you not see those are the eggs of a venomous snake? Would you hatch the young of a creature that would surely kill you?"

The Thrush

A little thrush spotted a myrtle bush covered in berries. Famished, she settled among the branched and began to feast. A bird catcher saw her, but she was too busy eating to notice. Stealthily, the bird catcher brought up a net and surrounded the thrush. Just as she was about to be caught, she cried out:

"I should have ignored my desire for pleasure! On this occasion it cost me my freedom!"

THE GNAT AND THE LION

Gnat thought himself the physical equal of all creatures and even claimed that he could fight a lion. To prove this he found the fiercest, strongest lion in all the land and challenged him to a battle. Lion was perplexed but duly agreed, but as he did so the gnat shot up his nose! Gnat bit Lion savagely inside his tender nose and then proceeded to bite him all over his face. Unable to destroy his tormentor without scratching his own face to pieces, enraged Lion surrendered.

Gnat told anyone who would listen of exactly how he had defeated the King of Beasts.

But a few days later, Gnat flew into a spider's web. As the spider advanced to made a meal of him, he cried miserably: "I defeated the strongest of the strong, yet now I lose my life to a mere spider!"

THE LIONESS AND THE VIXEN

Vixen was taking her fox cubs out for a walk in the woods, enjoying seeing them tumbling over one another and chasing insects. As she and the cubs came into a clearing, she came upon a lioness with her cub.

"What a pity that you only have one child," said Vixen.

"Yes, just one" replied the lioness. "But a child that will become a lion."

THE WOLF AND THE HERON

W olf was very pleased with himself. He had managed to sneak into the chicken run of the nearby farm and steal two fat chickens without the farm dogs waking from their afternoon rest. Now he was greedily devouring them both by the river bank, a drift of brown and white feathers all around him.

He was greedily gobbling his prize down, when one of the little bones stuck in his throat. No matter how hard he swallowed, it would not shift. He tried to cough, but that only made it worse. It was now unbearably painful!

On the other side of the river he saw Heron motionless in the water, fishing. He called out a strangled cry to Heron to come over to him. Heron flapped over and asked him what the matter was, as he could see from Wolf's face that something was wrong.

"If you could fish this little chicken bone out of my throat with your long beak, I will give you a present!" he choked.

Wolf opened his mouth wide and Heron reached his beak in and quickly fished out the offending bone.

"Well, what is my present?" asked Heron.

"Your life," replied Wolf. "You put your head into the jaws of a wolf and came out again unscathed. Now get lost!"

THE LION, THE FOX AND THE WOLF

Lion, the King of the animal kingdom, was gravely ill. He felt sure that he was going to die and so he called all his subjects to him to pay their last respects.

Wolf had always been envious of Fox's higher favour with Lion. He looked around him while he queued to see his ruler and seized his opportunity:

"I really thought that Fox would be here," he announced, making sure that everyone could hear. "I always thought Lion was a great hero in Fox's eyes. It seems that when the mighty have fallen, some just have no respect for them any more." Yet Wolf had failed to notice that Fox had come trotting in during his speech and now was stood at Lion's side. He heard Wolf's words. Looking straight into Lion's yellow eyes, he said in a very smooth, clear voice:

"My dear King, as soon as I heard that you were ill, I scoured the land to find you a cure. I am glad to tell Your Majesty that I have found one!"

"Fox, you are so good," murmured Lion. "Tell me your wondrous cure before it is too late."

"You must take the skin of a freshly slaughtered wolf and wrap it tightly around your body," said Fox, with a flash of pointed teeth.

Lion issued the command and Wolf was seized. Two bears marched him out to kill him. Fox called out:

"Funny how friends can find cures in their enemies faults."

THE SWAN MISTAKEN FOR A GOOSE

A merchant bought a swan and a goose from the market and kept them together in his courtyard. He wanted one bird for its famously beautiful song and the other to fatten up for his dinner table. Yet no matter how much he encouraged Swan, she refused to sing.

The merchant planned an extravagant feast. He commanded that the swan be brought before him to sing for his guests and the goose be caught and slaughtered for supper that night. The servant did not know which bird was which, so he grabbed one at random. This happened to be the swan. Sensed that she was about to be killed, Swan sang out a haunting lament. The servant immediately realised his mistake and let the swan go.

Hearing of this, the merchant remarked: "I was a fool to request that bird sang before, prepare her for sacrifice and my guests will enjoy fine entertainment before they dine!"

THE WILD BOAR
AND THE HORSE

Horse lived in a beautiful pasture by a river, with only a few sweet songbirds to keep him company. He was very happy and content until one evening he received a visitor. Wild Boar had swum across the river after catching the scent of the sweet apples that grew on the opposite bank. Grunting and shaking the water from his bristly hide, the boar walked over to the apple trees. He began scoffing up all the apples that lay on the ground. Horse wandered over to Boar, most indignant at being imposed upon by this unwanted guest.

"Excuse me, but what are you doing here? This is my pasture and those are my apples that you are eating," Horse said, as politely as he could.

"Well," Boar grunted through a mouthful of apple, "looks like there's plenty for everyone. I'm sure you don't mind if I help myself." He then returned to greedily scoffing apples.

After he had finished eating, the boar went to the riverbank and churned up the grass to make a mud wallow. Horrified, Horse asked him what he was doing and the boar replied: "Mud is very good for the skin you know. Keeps the flies away – you should try it!"

"No, thank you" said Horse tossing his head in annoyance. Now he would have to walk through all that mud, just to have a drink of water!

"So where are you on your way to then?" asked Horse.

"Don't rightly know," said the boar. "This is a pleasant spot. I might stay here a few weeks."

A few weeks! Horse knew he could not bear such vulgar company for one more day. The next morning (after a sleepless night due to Boar's snoring) Horse set off for the edge of the woods. He went straight to the huntsman's cabin. He told the huntsman about the boar being in his pasture and how he wanted it gone. The huntsman listened, nodding.

"Well, I cannot go after a wild boar on foot," the huntsman. "I shall have to ride upon your back to do this task for you. You shall have to wear a bridle and saddle."

"I understand. I am perfectly willing to become a hunting horse. I just want rid of him."

So the huntsman mounted Horse and together they hunted the boar and chased him for many miles. Eventually the huntsman got a clear shot and killed the beast. He slung the carcass over Horse's back and led him back to the cabin. He then led Horse round the side of the cabin and tethered him in the stable.

Hunting season had come to an end and for the rest of the summer Horse was forced to stay shackled in the shade, looking upon the idyllic pastures where he had once roamed free. If only he had been happy to share the pasture for a while!

THE CRAB AND HER MOTHER

"You look ridiculous walking sideways like that!" Crab scolded her child as they scuttled across the sand.

"Mother, if you can show me how to walk straight, I will do it,' replied her child.

Naturally Crab knew that she could not and apologised.

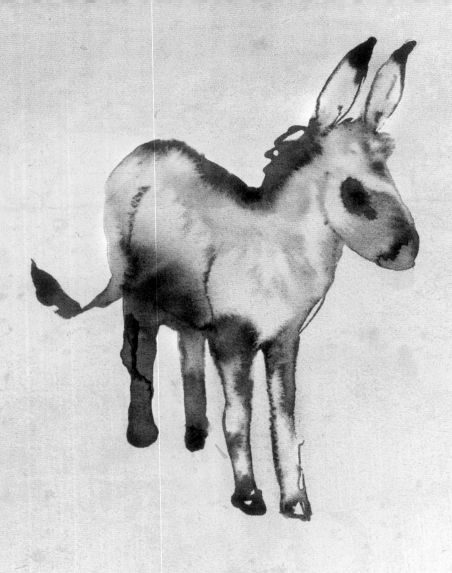

THE HORSE
AND THE DONKEY

Horse and Donkey were trudging along the dusty road to market, loaded up with goods to sell. Donkey stumbled and begged horse to share some of his burden. Horse refused:

"I'm no pack animal! I am the steed of great warriors in battle."

Further along the road, Donkey stumbled again and later collapsed and died.

The farmer loaded up Horse with not only all of Donkey's burden, but the dead body of Donkey too, to sell for glue in town. Horse regretted his refusal to help his more humble companion.

THE SLEEPING DOG AND THE WOLF

A little dog lay fast asleep in front of a grand house. Wolf was passing by and saw the dog. He pounced, but before he could gobble her up, she cried out:

"Don't kill me yet! I am all thin and stringy! My master is getting married soon and at the feast I shall be given all the leftovers. I shall get much fatter and tastier. Let me go this time and you shall have a feast next time you catch me."

So the wolf went on his way. A week later he returned, only to discover the clever little dog dozing on the roof of the house. She looked down at him and called out:

"I doubt you will catch me sleeping down there on the ground again! Next time I wouldn't wait for a wedding feast if I were you!"

THE ASS IN THE TIGER SKIN

Ass wandered into the house of a very wealthy merchant and saw a tiger skin rug spread out on the floor of the hall. He decided to play a trick. He threw the tiger skin over his back with the tiger's head covering his own head. He charged out of the house and onto the road. Every man, woman and child who saw him was utterly terrified and ran screaming away from him. He was so pleased with himself that he let out a long braying laugh. He did not notice Fox sitting calmly by the side of the road looking at him.

"If you could roar instead of bray," said Fox to the surprised ass, "you would not look quite so much like an ass right now."

The Lion, the Bear and the Fox

Lion and Bear met each other whilst out for a stroll in the fields. As they chatted they came across the body of a young deer. Lion reached out to grab it for his supper, but got knocked aside by Bear. They argued fiercely over who should have the carcass. Soon they were exchanging bites and claws and punches.

Meanwhile Fox came trotting out of the bushes and snatched up the carcass and carried it off. Lion and Bear did not notice until both of them were exhausted by fighting and had sat down. Some way off they spotted Fox feasting on the spoils of their fight. Both of them were too tired and sore to muster the energy to move.

"All this trouble," panted Lion. "To give Fox an easy supper!"

The Sun and the Frogs

There was great triumph and joy in the kingdom – Apollo, the God of the sun, was getting married! All the animals and men rejoiced, throwing great parties and dancing in the streets and fields and forests and seas.

The frogs, however, did not join in the celebrations. Instead, they sat looking glum in their marsh. When asked why they were not rejoicing too, the frogs replied:

"The Sun dries out our marsh every summer. If Apollo marries and has little baby suns, we will suffer without a home!"

THE ASS AND THE WOLF

Wolf was wandering through the fields to the woods when he saw Ass grazing nearby. Ass looked up and, catching sight of the vicious Wolf, began to limp away.

Wolf licked his lips in anticipation. He could not believe his luck. This was going to be a very easy meal indeed! He trotted up to Ass and asked him how he had injured himself.

"It is rather silly really," sighed Ass. "I was having a race with Mule and I ran over a big bramble and got a thorn caught in my hoof. I know that you are going to eat me, but first, for your sake, you'd better pull the thorn out. Otherwise you might choke on it."

Wolf agreed this was wise idea leant his face close to her hoof to find the thorn. Just then, Ass kicked Wolf hard with the very hoof he was examining! Wolf got half his teeth kicked out and winced in pain.

"Serves me right! I am a butcher, not a doctor!" said Wolf as Ass trotted away as fast as he could.

THE FOOLISH MONKEY KING

Monkey loved to dance and jest for all of the other animals. He made them all laugh so heartily and they liked him so much that they pronounced him their King.

Fox was very envious of Monkey's popularity and decided to trick him. He sidled up to Monkey and whispered, "My dear King! I have found treasure which, as royalty, is yours to take. Please follow me and I shall show it to you."

He led Monkey to a hunter's snare baited with some meat and told him that the meat was the treasure. Monkey, in his eagerness, reached out to take the meat and got caught in the trap.

"Foolish Monkey!" cackled Fox, "an idiot like you is not fit to be King of Beasts!"

THE TOWN MOUSE AND THE COUNTRY MOUSE

Country Mouse noticed that in the fields the barley and corn was ripening and the days were long and warm. He decided that now would be the best time to invite his cousin, Town Mouse to come and stay with him. Town Mouse arrived, looking very dapper and sophisticated, regaling his timid cousin with witty and thrilling stories. Country Mouse laid out a spread of the finest grain, roots and shoots that he could forage for their supper. Town Mouse nibbled them politely.

"Really, my dear cousin," he said, "you simply must come and sample the delights of my larder. My diet is delicious and varied. Why don't you come back to town with me and stay a while...escape this peasant existence and have a holiday!"

So Country Mouse accompanied his cousin back to town. The sights and smells were overwhelming, with people rushing this way and that. His cousin lived in a comfortable hole not far from the larder of a large and luxurious house. Supper time came around and they both scurried into the larder.

"See, there is bread and cheese and dried figs and apricots, cold cuts and jam, biscuits and beans!" reeled off Town Mouse to his awe-struck cousin. But before they could even begin to sample a mouthful, a red-faced cook bustled in. Poor Country Mouse's little heart was hammering! If they were seen, they would certainly be killed! The two mice had to hide in a very uncomfortable crack in the wall until she eventually left. Then they scampered out and began to feast. Not two minutes later a servant came in to fetch something and they had to hide again. They were interrupted no less than six times during the course of their hurried, but extravagant meal! After they had retired back to Town Mouse's hole, Country Mouse turned to him and said:

"What is the point in having such a feast, if there is no time to savour it? I would rather live peacefully in the country like a peasant, than like a lord in town, too terrified to enjoy my luxury!"

THE LION AND THE FROG

Lion was out taking an evening stroll. The breeze was warm, he had eaten a good supper and he was feeling content. Out of the stillness came a very load croak, which startled him out of his reverie.

Expecting a large creature to appear, he was astonished to see a frog crawling through the grass towards the spring:

"Less noise from one so small!" he growled and squashed the frog beneath his gigantic paw.

GREEDY FOX

Fox was ravenous. He had had no luck trying to catch rabbits and had worn himself ragged chasing after them. He was making his way back to his hole when he spied a fat bundle nestling in the hollow trunk of an old oak tree. He checked that nobody was around, then crawled inside and opened the bundle. He couldn't believe his luck! It was the farmer's lunch, packed with hearty and delicious food. Hastily, he devoured every last scrap.

However, he found as he tried to make his escape that his full belly was too fat to fit through the hole in the trunk! Crow, perched on the branches of the oak tree, saw Fox struggling to get out of the hole and called out to him:

"Relax and bide your time; wait until you go back to being thin, then I'm sure you can make your escape with no difficulty at all."

THE JACKDAW
AND THE PITCHER

The sun had baked the earth till it was cracked and dry and Jackdaw was thirstier than he had ever been in his life. His mouth was parched and his feet were sore from hopping about on the hot ground; he longed for a cool puddle to paddle in and drink from.

Resting in the shade of a tree, Jackdaw noticed a jug tucked in a hollow by the roots. Probably some young shepherd had left it there, but he wasn't in sight now. Jackdaw hopped over and peered into the jug. There was water in it! But he could not reach it with his beak. If he tipped over the jug, the water would spill out and instantly be swallowed up by the thirsty ground.

Then Jackdaw had an idea. He began picking up little rocks and stones and plopping them into the jug. Slowly the water level began to rise. Soon the level was high enough and Jackdaw was able to have his cool refreshing drink.

His desperation drove him to find a solution to his problem.

The Lion, the Ass and the Fox

Lion fell into conversation with Ass and Fox one evening when they were all drinking down by the river. Lion and Fox were praising one another's good points:

"You are such a skilful master of cunning. I am always impressed by your schemes," said Lion to Fox.

"As King of Beasts, you must have wondrous strength to wield such power," replied Fox.

"Well I've always been admirer of you both, so clever and so strong," brayed Ass.

The other two looked at Ass, but could find nothing to say to flatter him. He was always so foolish and looked ridiculous. Instead Lion said:

"It would be wonderful if all three of us went hunting together, do you think, Fox?"

"Absolutely!" said Fox. "What a team we'd make!"

They set off together. With the combination of brute strength, cleverness and foolhardiness, they managed to catch a large number of unfortunate birds and beasts.

Lion divided the spoils into two, the largest part for himself and a small part for Fox, knowing that Ass did not eat meat. Ass brayed in indignation that he wanted his share.

Furious, Lion pounced on him and killed him. Then he rounded on Fox: "I suppose you will be wanting a greater share too?"

"No, no, my dear Lion. I think you have done a perfect job! I learnt well from Ass that you do all things just right."

THE GNAT AND THE BULL

Gnat had grown weary of humming about the grass and decided to take a rest on the horn of a bull, who was grazing nearby.

After a while, feeling refreshed, he asked the bull whether he would mind if he left. The bull replied:

"I never noticed your arrival here so it really doesn't matter when or whether you come or go."

THE LION
AND THE DOLPHIN

Lion was walking along the seashore when he spotted Dolphin frolicking in the waves, chasing mackerel. He called out a greeting to him. Dolphin swam up to the rocks where he was standing and they started chatting.

"Really Dolphin, we would make the best team. You are King of the Sea and I am King of the Land. Together we could rule the world!"

They agreed to an alliance together and to help each other in every way. Lion came back to the seashore a few days later and asked Dolphin to help him in a war he had been in for a long time with a mighty wild bull. Dolphin said that he would of course help, but pointed out that he could not possibly leave the water.

"You are no true friend, Dolphin."

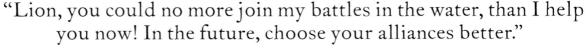

"Lion, you could no more join my battles in the water, than I help you now! In the future, choose your alliances better."

THE DANCING KID

Wolf saw a little kid was wandering away from its flock. He was hungry and made a lunge for his supper.

Clutched in Wolf's massive paws, Kid thought quickly. "Sir!" he cried, "before you devour me, let me dance one last time before you end my short life! There is the shepherd's flute – play and I shall dance for you."

Wolf saw no harm in this and began to play. Kid leapt and danced joyfully. However, the shepherd was nearby and heard the music. Walking nearer he saw the strange sight of Wolf piping and the dancing kid. He called out to his two sheepdogs and they quickly chased the wolf away.

As he fled, Wolf cursed himself. "I should have known better. I am a butcher, not a musician."

The Adder
and the Water Snake

Adder and Water Snake were at war. Adder infuriated Water Snake because he came to drink at the spring where she lived, invading her territory. Yet he would not let her come up onto the land without attacking her. They agreed to fight to the death and the victor would have control over both the land and the water.

The spring was also the home of a group of frogs. They hated Water Snake because she bullied and frightened their children. They timidly told Adder that they were on his side.

The battle began in earnest. It became clear that Adder was winning and the frogs set up a great chorus of croaking, cheering on his victory. Eventually Adder killed Water-Snake, then turned on the frogs, asking them why they did not help him.

"All you did was croak from the sidelines!" he cried.

"We are not warriors, but we sang you on your way to victory. That is all we are good for," replied the frogs.

THE HOUND AND THE HARE

Hound had pursued Hare for many miles. Eventually Hare tired and Hound caught him in his great paws.

Hound was panting and breathless from running about and could not bring himself to bite the hare. Instead, he lolled his great wet tongue over his catch.

Hare was terrified: "Do you want to bite me or kiss me?"

The Captured Eagle and the Fox

One day a hunter succeeded in trapping Eagle. He clipped his wings to stop him flying away, hoping to eventually train Eagle to hunt for him.

Eagle was so miserable; the Lord of the Skies, reduced to a pet! He hung his head in shame and refused to eat.

The hunter bored of this sickly creature and sold it to a merchant. The merchant, who had travelled far in strange lands, knew of the healing power of myrrh and rubbed it into the clipped quills of Eagle's wings. The wings grew back and Eagle soared and swooped into the air with pleasure. He caught a fine hare in his talons and presented it as a gift to the merchant. Fox saw all this and called out to Eagle:

"You should have given that hare to the hunter. Your merchant is a good caring man. The hunter only wants what he can gain. The present might stop him catching you and clipping your wings again!"

The Owl and the Birds

When the world was still very young, Owl, the wisest of all the birds gathered together all of her kind in order to share her wisdom. There were majestic rooks, long-legged herons, quiet curlews, white swans and cooing doves all craning their necks to hear her words. When the hubbub of chirruping and squawking and screeching had calmed down she spoke:

"I have three warnings for you all. It is imperative you listen, as your lives depend upon this." She lifted her wing to point to a young oak tree to her right.

"You see that young oak tree over there. One day it will have mistletoe growing upon it. As soon as you see the smallest sprout of this growing you must destroy it! This is because a sticky stuff called birdlime is made by it, which bird catchers will use to catch you!"

All the other birds looked at one another, thinking that maybe Owl was a little bit mad. But they kept listening.

"The second warning is that you must eat up any sprouts or seed of the flax growing in the grass. One day hunters will turn it into nets to catch you with!"

Now the other birds thought Owl really had lost it.

"The third warning is that you must hide away from any person seen carrying a bow and arrow like this," and she scratched a picture of it into the dirt. "They are your deadliest enemy. They will

128

fire an arrow, tipped with our feathers towards you when you are flying and kill you with one shot"

"You're crazy!" laughed the other birds and flew off.

Sure enough, all the things that Owl had warned them of came true. The birds begged her to impart her wisdom, but she refused. She lived alone and only went out at night, forever mournfully hooting the follies and foolishness of her kind.

THE HOUND, THE LION AND THE FOX

A hound had streaked ahead of the pack he was out hunting with and spotted Lion up ahead. He gave chase and lost all the other hounds. Lion quickly realised he was not being pursued by the whole pack, but only one hound and was quick to act. He turned and roared fiercely. The hound baulked and trembled. Fox, who was watching under some nearby trees called out:

"You gave chase alone to a fearsome lion, yet now you stop – because of his roar alone!"

THE HARES
AND THE FOXES

For many years a fierce battle had raged between the eagles and the hares. The eagles sharpened their talons and the hares stretched their long, muscular legs in preparation for the daily fight for survival.

As each day passed it became clearer and clearer that the hares were losing the fight. They were in need of an ally, so they pleaded with the clever foxes to help them.

The leader of the foxes came forward and spoke to the hares:

"We would help you, dear hares, but your enemy is too strong for us poor creatures to fight. If we joined you, we would certainly all be killed."

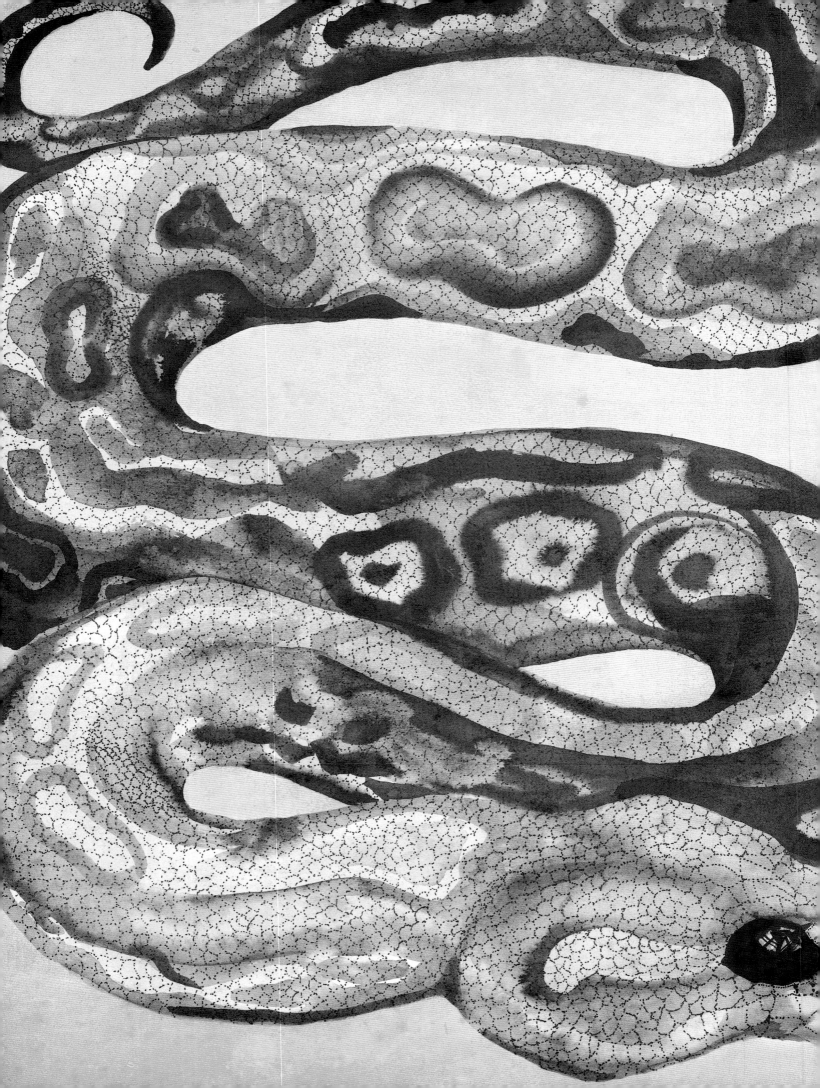

THE FOX AND THE GIANT SNAKE

Fox was trotting back to his hole when he spotted an enormous snake sleeping in the sun at the side of the path. It was huge! And it had laid itself out full length to get as much sun to warm its body as possible.

Fox wondered it he could make himself as long and impressive as this giant serpent. He stretched out his body on the grass, but try as he might he was smaller. With one final effort he stretched himself and the silly creature split himself in two.

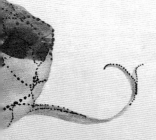

THE HORSE
AND HIS GROOM

A young groom kept his horse shining and glossy, brushing him attentively every day. He decided that because of his efforts he could cut down on the horse's feed, thereby making a profit on the leftover grain. As time went by, the horse got thinner and the coat that was once radiant was now patchy and dull.

"If you brushed me less and fed me more, I'd look as glossy as I did before," said the horse mournfully.

THE KITE'S CRY

Kite had a high keening cry that would cut through the air and terrify her prey. One day Kite heard a horse neighing in a field below where she flew.

She thought this sounded far better than her own cry and spent many days and nights trying to imitate the horse.

Despite all her efforts, Kite could never sound like a horse. In trying to neigh like a horse, she'd lost her own powerful cry.

THE LION AND THE MOUSE

It was the middle of the night and Lion had fallen into a deep sleep after a successful evening of hunting. As he lay dreaming, he felt a tickling across his belly. He reached out to scratch it but then felt it moving across his leg. Annoyed at having been woken, he opened his yellow eyes to see what was causing the tickle. With one paw he snatched up a tiny mouse.

"Please!" squeaked Mouse. "You fell asleep over the entrance to my home and I was trying to find it! If you do not squish me just yet, I will save your life one day." Amused by such words from such a tiny creature, Lion freed Mouse and moved so that he could scurry back to his hole, squeaking out with gratitude.

A couple of days later Lion got caught in a rope trap that had been set by some hunters. The more he struggled, the tighter the net wound itself around his body. Eventually he stopped struggling and fell, exhausted, onto the ground. After a couple of minutes he heard a squeak and the very same mouse scampered up onto his nose.

"I could not help you whilst you were struggling, but hold very still and I shall set you free." With that he began to nibble his way through the ropes of the net. It took quite some time but eventually, Lion was able to escape, freed by the tiny mouse.

The Snake, the Ferret and the Mice

Snake was making his way to the barn to hunt for mice for his supper. "I am so hungry," he thought himself, "I could eat at least thirty!"

Ferret was also on her way to the barn to hunt mice. "I am so hungry, she thought to herself, I could eat at least forty juicy mice!" Snake and Ferret caught sight of each other approaching the door of the barn and knew that they were both after the same thing.

"I am going to hunt here tonight!" said Ferret, bristling all over. "You go find somewhere else."

"No! I am staying – you are the one who has to leave!" hissed snake lashing his tail in irritation.

Ferret leapt at Snake and a fierce battle began. Fangs and teeth and claws and tails all whirled in a blur as they fought. The mice scuttled out to see the spectacle of their enemies fighting. Soon quite a crowd had gathered to look.

After a while Snake and Ferret stopped to catch their breath and they saw the mass of delicious spectators just sitting there. They looked at one another gleefully then rushed together at the mice. That night both Snake and Ferret ate their fill of mice.

THE WOLF AND THE HORSE

Wolf was on his way to the farmer's sheep pen to look for young lambs to steal for his supper. He crept stealthily across a field filled with deliciously ripe barley. A few fields along, he came across Horse and told him of the barley.

"I have been watching over it and watering it lovingly, because I know that you are so fond of it. But it is ready now for you to enjoy."

"Nonsense!" said Horse. "What lies you tell! If wolves could eat barley, you would not be messing about with such words."

With that he gave Wolf a sharp kick with his hoof and chased him off the farmer's land.

THE SILLY BILLY GOAT

Fox was unfortunate enough to slip and fall into a well. On realising he was stuck, he prepared himself for many cold and hungry nights spent all alone.

After a while, Billy Goat came trotting up the path. He was thirsty and had come to drink from the cool well. Looking over the edge, he saw two yellow eyes peering back at him.

"Oh! Hello there!" called out Billy Goat. "I say, dear fellow, is the water good in that well?"

"Why, yes!" called out devious Fox. "You must try it, there really is nothing sweeter! Jump down and when you've had enough I will help you out."

Billy Goat jumped down and drank and when he'd finished asked how they were going to get out.

"Well first you must brace your front legs against the wall, then I shall climb up you to get out. Once I'm out I shall get you out."

So the Billy Goat did as he was told and Fox scrambled up and out of the well.

"Me next! Help me out now!" said the goat.

Fox laughed out loud. "What a silly Billy! You should never get into a situation that you don't know how to get out of!"

THE ROYALTY OF THE LION

There was a time when a great Lion became King. He was good to the very depths of his heart. He was a just ruler over all the other animals and believed strongly in truth and fairness.

He made a royal decree that while he remained monarch there would be equality among all the animals, so that no creature need live in fear. He commanded that mortal enemies become friends and protect one another. Dog should protect Hare, Tiger protect Deer and Wolf guard over timid Lamb.

It was a golden age of peace and prosperity in the animal kingdom.

THE WILD GEESE AND THE CRANES

There were great expanses of wetlands where the river spread out before flowing into the sea. All kinds of bird from all over the world would congregate on the wetlands to forage for fish and insects in the marshes. The cranes would hunt only as much as they needed to sustain themselves, while the wild geese would gorge themselves until they were plump and fit to burst.

One day the wild geese were foraging near to the cranes, who were fishing in the shallow water. A pack of wild dogs had come out to the wetlands to hunt and spotted the group of birds. One of the cranes spotted the dogs as they came near and made a cry of alarm, before launching herself into the air. The cranes, with their lithe frames, were able to fly away quickly. However the geese, owing to much fatter bodies, were not so quick to make their escape and were caught by the dogs.

The Two Cockerels
and the Eagle

Two cocks fought over the hens, causing feathers to fly up and scatter across the yard. After many more feathers had been scattered the victorious cockerel flew high onto the wall to crow his triumph.

Little did he know it would be so short-lived. Perched high above the other birds it was not hard for Eagle to spot Cockerel, snatch him in her talons and carry him off to feed her chicks.

The defeated cockerel cautiously crept out from his hiding place and seeing all danger had passed, strutted happily up to join his hens.

The Chough
and the Raven

Ravens foretell bad omens. If a man sees a raven, he knows that Death cannot be far behind.

Little Chough wished that he held a position of such importance in the minds of others. He resolved to gain some status, so when he saw some travellers passing him by he let out a few sharp cries. The travellers were startled, but quickly relieved:

"No fear, it is only a silly little chough!" they cried.

THE VIPER AND THE FOX

Viper was slithering his way through the grass when he was swept away by a flash flood. He managed to wind himself onto a patch of thorny brambles that had also been swept away by the water.

Fox was sitting up on some high ground out of the way and spotted the viper drifting past.

"What a fitting vessel for such creature," he mused.

The Bull and the Wild Goats

Bull had been chased by Lion through the fields and into the hills. Rounding a bend, he saw a cave hidden on a small track up above. He scrambled up the little path and hid inside the cave before Lion reached the bend.

Inside the cave it was very dark and gloomy and before Bull's eyes adjusted, he felt something butt him hard on his flank. Then a kick came from another direction. It was a flock of wild goats kicking and butting him. He could now see them in the dark huddled at the back of the cave.

"Quiet down!" said Bull to the flock. "I can endure your blows, but they won't do you any good. Outside there is a much greater enemy, who will have all our skins if he hears us."

The Ageing Lion and the Fox

Lion was coming towards the end of his days and was finding it harder and harder to catch his food. His poor old paws could not keep up with the swift feet of a deer and he lacked the strength to catch a cow.

He decided that although his years had made him weaker, they had also made him wiser. He announced that he was feeling unwell and was going to retire to a cave in the mountainside. On hearing this, all the other creatures who had previously fled from him rejoiced, assuming that he was dying.

Each day someone was sent to see if the old Lion was still alive. Lion would wait in the cave and pounce on the creature that came into the cave to see him, whether it was large or small. Some days he was lucky and had a feast, others he only got a little rabbit. One day it was Fox's turn to go check on Lion. He trotted up to the cave, but stopped some distance from its entrance. He called out:

"Lion, How are you feeling today?"

"Not very well at all," groaned Lion. "I have a terrible backache, would you come and rub it for me?"

"I'm afraid I cannot," said Fox. "You do not treat your visitors well. I can see many sets of footprints coming in to see the patient, but find it very strange that none of these footprints show your visitors leaving."

THE WOLVES AND THE SHEEP

A pack of wolves were trying to steal sheep from a flock on the hillside, but kept being foiled by the sheepdogs guarding the flock. They knew that the only way to get the sheep was through some form of sly trickery.

In the darkest part of night, one of the young wolves was sent to relay a message to the sheep:

"My wolf pack wish to make friends with you sheep," he said. "But the sheepdogs are jealous and do not want us to become friends. We have planned a wonderful party for you all in the woods over there, but the dogs would never let you come. If you sneak through that little gap in the fence there, you can join us and we can all make merry until it is dawn. Then you can sneak back and the sheepdogs need never know a thing! It can be our little secret."

The sheep always thought what a bossy lot the sheepdogs were and how they never had any fun. They decided that a party in the night would be great fun, so each and every sheep sneaked through the gap in the fence and made their way towards the woods.

But as each of the silly sheep went into the trees, they were pounced on and quickly made into a hungry wolf's dinner.

The Antelope and the Lion in the Cave

Antelope was exhausted, having been chased through fields, woods and even farms by huntsmen. On the side of a steep hill she was relieved to see a cave and leapt up to it. Yet, rather than escaping danger she ran straight into another threat. Once inside, she came face to face with Lion, who seized her in his claws.

"How could I have known?" she cried, "that the dangers I fled would throw me into the jaws of a beast even more terrifying than arrows and spears?"

THE CAT AND THE HENS

One day the farmer went out to see his hens, only to find them all terribly ill and decided to call the vet.

Cat, who overheard, was famished and dressed himself up as a vet with a neat leather case for all his medicines. He approached the hens, who started to shriek:

"Stay away! Whatever ails us is not nearly as bad for us as your 'cure', you fiendish Cat!"

THE WOLF AND THE LION

A flock of sheep were being moved from one pasture to another. Wolf, watching from afar, had hidden himself in a hedge to lie in wait for when they passed. He saw a particularly fat lamb, trotting some distance from its mother. As it passed, he leapt out and grabbed it in one swift movement without anyone noticing. As he was trotting back to the woods with the dead lamb in his jaws he met Lion:

"For me?" asked Lion in mock surprise. "Oh Wolfie dear! You really shouldn't have!" Lion seized the lamb and began to devour it right then and there.

"Hey, Lion! That's not fair! You know that was mine," cried out Wolf.

"You got this gift by fair means, I'm sure," growled Lion between mouthfuls. "So it is only fair that I get this gift from you."

THE HARES AND THE FROGS

The hares decided to hold a meeting to discuss their troubles. Each and every one of them cried and trembled, telling the company of how they had been hunted as prey by humans, dogs, eagles, foxes, wolves, cats, ferrets...the list was endless! How unfair it was that they were an easy supper for so many terrifying creatures, how unjust that they should live their lives in fear. Why, their little hearts pounded just talking about it!

They wound each other up so badly that they all decided it was really best to put an end to their suffering. They all rushed together to a nearby pond to drown themselves. A group of frogs resting on the rocks at the edge of the pond were so alarmed by the charge of hares that they leapt away into the water as fast as they could. Seeing this, the lead hare shouted out:

"Wait! Here in this pond are creatures are greater cowards than us. They find us terrifying! These poor frogs live in greater fear than us. There is always someone worse off than yourself."

THE ASS AND THE CICADAS

A ss was lazing about in a meadow listening to the wonderful summer song of the cicadas. He asked them what diet they ate to give them such wonderful voices, so that he might sing like them.

"We drink the dew every morning," they chirruped.

Silly Ass was desperate to sound beautiful and decided he only drink dew for the rest of the summer.

It was not long before he starved.

THE CAMEL AND ZEUS

Camel was out walking when he saw Bull grazing in a nearby field. He saw that Bull was blessed with a most splendid pair of horns. He went to Zeus, King of the Gods and asked if he might have horns too.

"Are you not content with your huge size and strength, Camel? You should appreciate what has been given to you"

As punishment Zeus shrunk the size of Camel's ears, which looked ridiculous next to his huge hump.

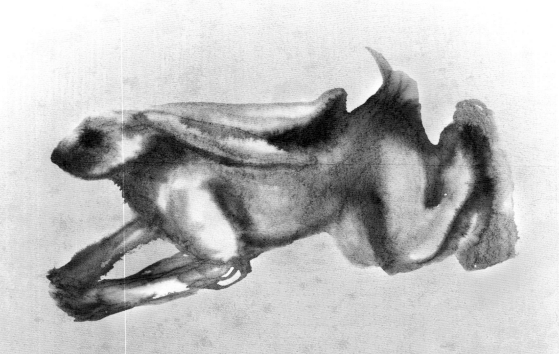

THE LION AND THE HARE

Hare felt sleepy in the heat of the day. He had frolicked all morning and felt he had earned a rest, so he decided to nap under a tree.

As Hare lay sound asleep in the grass Lion came prowling past and saw him. "What an easy meal a young, sleeping hare would be," he thought to himself.

But as he was about to spring, he saw a deer down at the bottom of the meadow. He leapt over Hare's sleeping body and gave chase. Hare awoke to the sound of Lion's bounding paws and streaked as far away as he could. Lion chased the deer but soon grew tired, as the afternoon sun was beating down upon his back. Panting, he padded back to where Hare had been sleeping, but discovered that both possible meals had escaped.

"I should have been content with an easy meal," he muttered.

THE HEN THAT LAID THE GOLDEN EGGS

The farmer and his wife were blessed. They had a wonderful brood of chickens who all laid beautiful large eggs every day. But this was not the reason for their fortune. They had one hen which was truly special, for it laid eggs of solid gold. The farmer and his wife grew rich very quickly as the hen laid a golden egg each and every day. They sold the farm and bought a huge house, had servants and many fine horses. The wife had divine dresses and piles of jewels and the farmer had beautifully tailored clothes. They kept the hen well fed in a chamber with a few other hens to keep her company and she continued to lay a golden egg every day. One day, the wife said to her husband:

"What if that hen of ours is filled to the brim with gold? If we opened her up we would be richer than kings or emperors! We could rule the world with all the gold that must be inside that hen!"

The farmer thought his wife's idea was very clever. He dreamt of all the wonders he could achieve with that much gold.

So they went to the hen coop and cut open her little body with a sharp knife. They of course discovered she was not filled up with gold and inside she was just like any other chicken. The hen that laid the golden eggs was mourned by her brood and the farmer and his wife were no longer able to afford all their luxuries.